EDGES

Earthshake

Book 4

Bjorn Esterday Was Not Born Yesterday

Wynter Sommers

GJ dePillis

USA Copyright © 2017 Susan E dePillis & GJ dePillis

TXu001885818
PAu 3-627-478, 1-798104171, PAu003401882, PAu003759141, 1-787-353831
Library of Congress Control Number: 2019930922

Published by Pure Force Enterprises, Inc.
California, USA
Since 2002

ISBN-13: 978-1-7184-0005-4
ISBN-10: 1-7184-0005-5

DEDICATION

To all of us whose hearts reach out to change the world around, whose minds calculate the next strategic move, whose souls crave adventure and value freedom of democracy. To the spirit harnessing the power of fiction to alter our reality, making the world a better place for everyone.

Bjorn Esterday Was Not Born Yesterday Series

Firebrand (9 Stories +Conversation Station Book)
Edges (9 Stories +Conversation Station Book)
Gone (18 Stories + 2 Conversation Station Books)

Bjorn EDGES Series
EDGES Book 1-Swift Encounter
EDGES Book 2-Rousing Attack
EDGES Book 3-One Foot Under
EDGES Book 4-Earthshake
EDGES Book 5-Broken String
EDGES Book 6-Key Witness
EDGES Book 7-Who is She?
EDGES Book 8-Vanish
EDGES Book 9-Chase or Die

Bjorn Series Alternate Reading Plan

1st   Edges Book 1
2nd   Edges Book 2
3rd   Gone Book 1
4th   Firebrand Book 1
5th   Edges Book 3
6th   Firebrand Book 2
7th   Gone Book 2
8th   Gone Book 3
9th   Firebrand Book 3
10th   Gone Book 4
11th   Firebrand Book 4
12th   Gone Book 5
13th   Gone Book 6
14th   Edges Book 4
15th   Firebrand Book 5
16th   Gone Book 7
17th   Firebrand Book 6
18th   Gone Book 8
19th   Firebrand Book 7
20th   Gone Book 9
21st   Firebrand Book 8
22nd   Gone Book 10
23rd   Gone Book 11
24th   Gone Book 12
25th   Gone Book 13
26th   Firebrand Book 9 (End)
27th   Gone Book 14
28th   Gone Book 15
29th   Gone Book 16
30th   Gone Book 17
31st   Gone Book 18 (End)
32nd   Edges Book 5
33rd   Edges Book 6
34th   Edges Book 7
35th   Edges Book 8
36th   Edges Book 9 (End)

CONTENTS

ACKNOWLEDGMENTS

To all those gentle souls who have graciously given tokens of love, hope, and kind considerations to others.

0 Preface

Previously, we saw a flashback in which Jack Courtly and his brother Skipper have a disagreement right before Jack and his family board the Courtly train for a family vacation.

After the train hostages are corralled on the ground outside, they encounter a spray of AnCor bullets and Widow Medicina collapses. Does she die because of a heart attack, or getting shot, or does anyone, terrorized hostages or murderous AnCors, even care ?

Percy Snatcher proclaims his power and leadership over the local AnCor cell in the AnCor camp.

When Slash returns to camp after having been chased by the Soldier Police of Courtly City, Percy is wary that their secret location may have been compromised. Slash, ever devoted, assures Percy otherwise.

1 CHAPTER- Year 2036: Remodeling (Continuous Ch 33)

Rigging and construction vehicles went into operation all over the grounds of Skipper's newly purchased castle, as full-time restoration of the building and its gardens began. Pip and his father Skipper walked around the grounds assessing what should to be done and how much it would cost.

Pip and Skipper headed inside the castle to find workmen puzzling over a set of blueprints. Both overheard their workers talking and approached slowly.

"The staircase is right there," said one construction worker pointing to the stone steps leading downward, "but it's not on the blueprints."

"Well," the other man replied, "maybe those stairs were added later and the updated blueprints were never filed."

"Stone steps? It's part of the foundation. Old enough to be part of the original design," the first construction worker protested.

The heavy front door was propped open, letting bugs fly in. Skipper swatted at a couple of the insects as he continued to eavesdrop, listening intently.

"We should just go down and check it out to see if whatever is downstairs will support the weight of what we are building on this level."

"Good idea," the other said as they both headed toward the staircase.

"Stop!" Skipper barked at the two

construction workers. "Nobody goes down that stairway! That means you. That means any of the other workers, here. You were hired to remodel from this level up," Skipper scolded.

A foreman seeing his customer, Skipper Courtly, upset, hurried over to investigate as the other workers simply melted away and got busy on another job.

The foreman respectfully addressed Skipper. "Mr. Courtly, Sir, my men thought we should see whatever is down that stairway because it's not on our blueprints of this building. We just want to know if there is anything structurally unsound with the foundation that might damage the remodeling we are doing to the upper levels. That's all. Please, Sir. Feel free to come with us, if you like."

"No! Nobody goes down," Skipper insisted.

"There seems to be several places that you don't want us to inspect before we build."

The Foreman hesitated, then produced a short waiver. "Sir, may I ask you to please sign this?"

"What is it?" Skipper snapped.

"You see, sir," the foreman started, "it's all written right there."

"I don't have my reading glasses! Just tell me what it says!" Skipper demanded.

The foreman hesitated. "Yes, sir. It states you understand that you are declining inspection."

"And?" prompted Skipper, "What else?"

"You understand," the foreman continued looking at the pages, summarizing them, "that there are areas in this structure that you are preventing us from inspecting. Without an inspection, sir, we cannot determine if your upper floors can be supported by the foundation. If there is rot, termites, or inadequate materials, you assume full responsibility. You agree to not sue us, sir. You agree to not expect our company to make unpaid-for repairs. And, sir, you agree to pay us in full for all work we have bid on." The foreman, proffering a writing implement, looked nervously at Skipper.

Annoyed, Skipper scribbled his signature on the document. "Stay upstairs. Period."

2 CHAPTER Year 2032: Widows' Cloister (Continuous Ch 34)

Inside the Widows' Cloister inner courtyard, well-manicured gardens bloomed with both beautiful and edible delights. Vines produced shiny ripe tomatoes. Grape tendrils wound around trellises. Apple branches weighed down with abundant firm fruit. Small pink picnic rose bushes and large white moondance roses were in full flower. Delicately colored double-bloom Peonies, or Paeoniaceae, accented splashes of color amongst rows of neat tulips. Just outside the stone building, but still within its protective walls, were trees and bushes filled with abundant fruits and vegetables.

"Widows" worked with loving diligence alongside "sisters", who were those who had lost their families, yet never married. Both widows and sisters were here at the Widows' Cloister because they had suffered irreparable losses in their families. They healed their broken hearts by working joyfully alongside their companions.

An older Earth Farmer, tenderly called "Eldress", managed the Widow's Cloister. All the women pooled their skills to create a self-sustaining community, which traded goods on Market Day. This was a safe and happy place to mourn their losses and start a new chapter in their lives.

Queenie Courtly, two years after the train hijacking, was now gardening, dressed in simple Earth Farmer garb. Her crop this season was most abundant. She was just harvesting a new batch of apples to make into simple apple pies. One of the other widows had traded just last week for sugar, butter, and flour.

Queenie had learned her baking skills and gardening while here in the cloister. Her pies were a welcomed treat when apples were in season.

One of the sisters called cheerfully, "May I have one before you bake it?" as she passed by wearing paint splattered work pants, holding a paint brush and pail in one hand.

"Of course," Queenie said. "This variety should be especially sweet and best when eaten fresh."

Queenie plucked a nicely ripened fruit from the tree, tossing an apple to the sister.

"Thanks!" The sister caught it from across the courtyard as she headed toward a widow who was setting up a ladder along the façade.

"This will give me enough energy to finish patching that wall," the sister smiled.

"Here's another one for Widow Salina up there on that ledge." Queenie pitched the fruit baseball-style.

The sister smiled, "Hey," she said victoriously when she caught it, "I guess Proverbs 3:27 to 29 is really true in this case."

She put the second apple in her pocket and took another juicy bite of the fruit she held in her hand.

"Eh?" Queenie prompted.

"You know, Widow, Honor the Lord with...the best part of everything you produce. Then he will fill your barns..."

"Oh, right!" Queenie smiled and turned back to her harvesting work.

The first sister scampered off, calling to the woman who had set up the ladder and was already ascending with a paint brush in her teeth.

"I got an apple for you!" sang the first sister from the ground, peering up as the other woman looked down, unable to speak because of the paint brush handle in her mouth.

Once she crept onto a narrow ledge where paint cans were waiting, she put the paint brush down, and leaned precariously over the edge with both hands open, ready to catch. The first sister tossed Queenie's bright apple up and Widow Salina caught it.

"Thanks!" she called down to Queenie after she took a bite of it.

"My pleasure, Widow!" Queenie called back as she smiled at the sight of these two women making repairs. This cloister was their home and they all pitched in to keep it looking nice.

Things were always breaking down and the sisters had to learn to be self-sufficient to keep it running. With the constant patching and repainting, the building didn't look as old as it really was. Fortunately, it had been constructed during a time when architects wanted their buildings to last for hundreds of years. This one did. But, it needed continual maintenance.

Queenie was happy here, except for one thing. She could only remember the last two years of her life, and those years had been spent in this Cloister.

From across the gardens, the Eldress was escorting a visitor from the city. They both turned as the Eldress pointed to Queenie.

"There she is," smiled the Eldress.

"Oh?" the visitor commented, "that's not my aunt." The visitor looked at the other widows and sisters in the garden, "None of these women look remotely like my aunt."

"But, the one by the apple trees is Widow Medicina. She has been here for a couple of years," the Eldress persisted as she squinted at Queenie.

"No. My aunt is a very short woman, like my mother. About five foot tall. That woman is much taller and thinner than my aunt could ever hope to be." The visitor looked sadly disappointed.

"I'm so sorry, Child," the Eldress comforted. "Perhaps our records are wrong. Perhaps your Widow Medicina is in a different cloister. We don't keep electronic records, you see."

"I understand," the young visitor stated simply. "I am disappointed, but I will keep looking for my mother's sister. Thank you for your patience, Eldress."

The Eldress nodded quietly and guided the visitor out.

A short time later, the Eldress returned to the gardens and stood at a distance, observing Queenie.

Queenie smiled as the Eldress approached and sat on a stone bench.

"Widow dear, can you stop for a moment and sit by me?" Eldress invited.

Queenie stopped placing fruits into her baskets and sat next to the older woman on the bench.

"My dear. I wish we knew your name."

"We've been over this a hundred times, Eldress. You said you were expecting a Widow Medicina, so that has to be my name," Queenie gently protested.

"Yes. I believe the Widow Medicina we were preparing for may have been older and shorter than you. And remember, you had no identification when Elder James brought you to us. We can't even be sure you are a widow." Eldress paused briefly, then added softly, "I'm so sorry..."

"You said I had a wedding ring on when I arrived."

"A widow has a dead husband. All I know is that you were married," the Eldress replied.

"If my husband were alive, wouldn't he have called for me by now?" Queenie asked.

"He may not know where you are," the Eldress sighed deeply as she continued, changing her tone. "After two years, it does please me to see that you appear to be truly content, here."

Queenie smiled, "I am."

"But," Eldress went on, "Is this really the life God has for you? I have been

15

praying, Child, and I wonder if perhaps there is another path for you to follow?"

"Another path?" Queenie shook her head, "Eldress, are donations down? I know this place is always in a state of disrepair, but we all chip in to fix it... Are you trying to tell me that you cannot afford to keep me?"

Worry brushed across Queenie's brow.

The Eldress gave Queenie a shoulder hug, "Of course not, Child. The only ones who should fear the future are those who plot evil schemes." Then she quoted, "The fears of the wicked will all come true; so will the hopes of the godly. Proverbs 10:24."

"You mean I need to find out what special gift God gave me?"

"Oh Child," the Eldress sighed, "...the gifts God bestows are not what you enjoy doing, but what others keep asking you to do. You know that." She gazed at Queenie earnestly, "Your hopes will come to pass in His good timing."

"His timing is never fast enough," Queenie suggested.

"And that is why we need patience, Child." The Eldress smiled tenderly, "I want you to promise me to pray about finding the path that God wants for you." She looked at Queenie.

"My path? I'm happy here," Queenie simply stated.

"If you knew your past and freely chose this vocation of your own informed free will, I would support your decision to remain. However, you are here today because you were found wounded by Elder James. Your days before coming here two years ago are still a mystery." Eldress patted Queenie on the hand. "Trust in the Lord God with all your heart and do not depend on your own understanding. Seek to do His will in all your actions and He will show you which path to take. Proverbs 3:3 through 5."

"I do seek His will. I have prayed. I haven't gotten any answers," Queenie exclaimed. Tears stung her eyes.

"Child," Understanding Queenie's fear, Eldress reassuringly said, "I want you to know that until you hear from God through the circumstances he presents to you, you will always be welcomed to stay with us at the Cloister. And of course, I pray you have discernment to recognize those opportunities. Remember, God never shouts. He whispers. Read the Good Book and pray daily."

Suddenly, Elder James burst through the gates. He was frightfully apologetic and obviously harried.

"Eldress, I am so sorry for my unannounced intrusion." He lowered his head in deference. "We have heard your crops are abundant and ours are not. We don't have enough food for all the prisoners we minister to. Could we impose on you to share of your abundance and provide food for the prisoners who don't have families to bring them a meal?"

3 CHAPTER   Year 2032: Men's Prison (Continuous Ch 35)

The prison, heavily guarded by Courtly Prison Guards, was a large network of underground tunnels which had been converted from a now defunct manufacturing plant. Convicts were not allowed to have sharp razor blades, so all the men were bearded. Every so often, they could be groomed and it was considered a perk to be sent to the barber to get clean shaven or have your beard trimmed. The prison cells were dingy and dirty.

Those in uniform were the guards.

The jailbirds wore what they came in with. Occasionally, Earth Farmers, as part of their godly obligations to show kindness to these prisoners, made a commitment to feed and clothe them .

Inside the walls, Elder James, in his simple Earth Farmer garb, handed out food to the hungry prisoners. Overseeing

19

the inmates, who were now gobbling the food handed out by Elder James, was Guard Gene. He had silently observed Elder James on his frequent visits to the prison.

Two years had passed since the AnCors had left Guard Gene for dead on the train. He was proud to be part of the organization that had come after him, and safely extracted him from the hidden AnCor camp, when it would have been cheaper to have left him for dead. Today, he wore an eye patch and brutal scar on his face, as a reminder of that day.

"Your compassion for this filth seems sincere..." Always suspicious, Guard Gene addressed Elder James as he tapped his scar. "An AnCor gave me this, and when I was on the edge of death, wanted to still sell me as a slave. If it were up to me, I'd let them starve."

"Not all the men here are AnCors, Officer," Elder James reminded him. "But, I do understand your bitterness and resentment."

Elder James walked along to offer a bit

more food to a couple of prisoners near him.

"I thank you, Officer Gene, for letting me feed these men. Not all of them have families to drop off food."

Elder James smiled at Jack Courtly, now bearded and looking haggard. "Do you have family outside, my son?"

"No. I don't," Jack muttered.

Elder James gave him an extra-large portion and smiled, sad that Jack was denied the joys of a loving family. Then, he started to clean and pick up the now empty baskets he had brought.

Jack jumped up, and walked quickly to Elder James, saying, "I thank you for the meal, sir. May I help so you won't need to make two trips to load your cart before the curfew signal?"

Elder James, tired after a long day, was appreciative of the offer.

"Yes, friend, provided the guards are agreeable." Both Jack and Elder James turned toward Guard Gene.

"Sure...go ahead. Help pack up," Gene replied, "but remember the second whistle is the curfew. If you don't get out before the second whistle, you'll be locked in for the night and you will not be allowed back to the prison afterwards."

Jack proceeded to efficiently gather everything Elder James needed.

"If you could help me bring these outside, friend..." Elder James asked Jack with his arms full, "...My horse is just out there."

He indicated the yard outside the building, but still within the prison walls.

Jack and Elder James, arms overloaded so they wouldn't need to make a second trip, went outside the door to see the silhouette of Elder James' horse-drawn wagon against the dusky sky.

Sitting inside the cart, waiting, were two passengers, which Jack could barely make out. He couldn't tell if these shapes were men or women, just that they were patiently waiting for the return of Elder James.

They had remained in the cart during his entire ministry, so Jack assumed they must be women. Women wouldn't be allowed inside the halls of a men's prison, especially not an Earth Farmer woman. One wouldn't want to expose her to grotesque uninvited attentions of the already depraved men.

Guards were patrolling the area at the exit of the compound to ensure Elder James left the premises before the entire complex went into lock-down.

Then, the shut-down whistle blew. The shrill wail was the signal that in a few moments, Elder James had better get out. He quickened his pace to load up his cart.

"Before I came here today," Elder James explained to Jack as he sped up, "I realized we didn't have enough food. So, I stopped by the Widow's Cloister to supplement our supplies. I'm afraid that delay has made me quite late. I must be gone before the second whistle and obey their rules. We must hurry to load these supplies or the guards may not permit me to return."

In his haste, Elder James tripped. Gasps were heard from the silhouettes in the cart as the empty baskets Elder James' was carrying rolled out onto the ground. Jack raced to the back of the cart and placed his supplies in, then returned to help Elder James.

"Widow Medicina, help Elder James, while I ready this steed for a speedy departure," Sister Prudence told Queenie. Queenie hopped down from the wagon quickly to help Elder James and Jack clean up.

In the dimming light, Jack stared at this woman who was assisting them. Jack's hand accidentally brushed against hers. Queenie, frightened, pulled her hand away.

"It's me. Jack!" he whispered to Queenie as Elder James hurried to pack up the cart and leave, "Look at me. Don't you know who I am?" Jack whispered hoarsely.

At that moment Elder James called for Queenie. "Widow Medicina, we must fly now!" and Queenie sprinted back to the cart, barely getting on board as the cart and its passengers raced through the gates as they were closing. Soldier Police guards were shouting at them to hurry up and get out. The massive doors slammed shut behind them.

The horse would have to be driven hard that night, to drop off the ladies at the Widow's Cloister before he returned to the Earth Farmer monastery.

Then, the second whistle blew.

4 CHAPTER Year 2032: Earthshake (Continuous Ch 36)

From inside the prison, one Soldier Police guard raced out, shouting an order to get Jack back into his cell.

Quickly, Jack obeyed.

As he briskly marched to his cell, Jack replayed the last few moments in his head. Was it a coincidence that some Earth Farmer woman looked like Queenie? Did she survive that train hijacking?

If it was Queenie, did she recognize him? She had never seen him with a beard, dirty, in shabby clothes, but surely she must have recognized Jack's voice. Why didn't Queenie speak to him? Or maybe it wasn't Queenie at all. Maybe this was just a fantasy his mind concocted to help him cope with his imprisonment.

Jack recalled that when he was being processed by the guards on his first day at the prison, he had confidently announced, "You've made a mistake. I'm Jack Courtly."

"Oh? You mean this guy whose brother is holding a funeral service for?" The processing guard's expression hardened and he peered closely at Jack. The guard indicated a picture in the news of Skipper Courtly attending the funeral, mourning the death of his brother, Jack.

After a few attempts, Jack began to realize that for his own survival in this prison, he had better become anonymous.

Jack became so twisted in these circles of thought that he didn't realize the mood of his fellow prisoners seemed more anxious than normal. Something was in the air. Jack hurried back to his cell.

At the same time, a few miles away, as the horse drawn cart approached the Widow's cloister, Queenie had become absorbed in her own thoughts.

For some reason, this trip to the men's prison gave Queenie much to think about. She didn't even participate in the conversation that Elder James and Sister Prudence were having. They discussed the types of food the prisoners liked; which prisoners got news from the outside about a family member; how well behaved they are when Elder James arrives. One was even helpful this time to aid him in packing up.

Elder James always had hope for a character change in these inmates.

Back inside his cell, Jack Courtly still pondered this odd occurrence. If he had never offered to help Elder James pack up, he never would have encountered this woman. If Elder James' food supply had not been depleted, he would not have stopped by the Widow's cloister to collect more food and need the assistance of these women... and if Elder James had not tripped, Jack would not have seen the setting sun highlight the features of a woman who looked just like Queenie.

Jack was driven by an ardent desire to find out the truth. Jack was either a fool for thinking this woman was Queenie or perceptive in identifying her. If it were Queenie, Jack would have something to live for. The possibility of his wife being alive turned his thoughts from black and white into color. Somehow, he had to get an informant to go to the Widow's cloister and find out who that woman was.

Jack's thoughts were interrupted by the hushed excited voices of prisoners nearby.

The first prisoner said, "I got word they're letting us out. So, then I can manage the troops."

The other replied, "Where will they set us up? What do you mean 'lead the troops'? I think the men would follow me...Not you..."

"What about that Earth Farmer Cloister?" The first prisoner offered.

"It's filled with women, but it's a great location. Just imagine, one day if Percy Snatcher could get out and take that place over..."

"Right! Get rid of those women! Take over. We'd have the best AnCor camp around. And then, I become the leader of our group. So long Percy Snatcher!"

"Percy would never let you take over if we ever got out of here. Just get to sleep." The AnCor buried his head under his pillow.

Jack listened motionless.

A low rumble, barely felt, grew into something that sounded like a loud rolling thunder. Then snapped. Then, glass buckled, objects clattered to the ground, and cabinets swung open.

"Earthshake! Earthshake!" Came the cries.

"Is this part of the plan? Hey, What's going on?" the prisoner shouted as his pillow dropped to the floor.

Alarms went off.

Guards rushed in, then took cover themselves. Prisoner adrenaline skyrocketed and tensions mounted as the prisoners took this chance to push on doors and buckling walls to get out of their cells.

Parts of the ceiling started to collapse in on them.

Pipes burst, spewing out valuable water, flooding paths of escape.

Jack, saw his chance to get out, as did other inmates. Some overpowered guards and broke into the armory. A bloodthirsty frenzy overtook these men, who but an hour ago, were docile eating their supper.

Then another SNAP and more debris poured from the ceiling. It was an AfterShake. Then another slow rumbling shook the walls. The ground rolled beneath their feet like a freshly snapped bed sheet, tossing them off balance.

Jack raced away from the mounting riot and took a side tunnel, avoiding precarious debris as it fell around him.

He took a sharp turn and suddenly came face to face with Guard Gene. One of the prisoners he heard earlier plotting to take over, held a weapon at Guard Gene, who had been disarmed. The guard stood with his hands up.

The prisoner didn't see Jack at first and simply focused through the sites of the weapon muttering, "Payback."

Jack immediately saluted this ego-centric prisoner in such an exaggerated manner, that he had to look at Jack.

"The others sent me to tell you that they want you to lead the men, Sir! Go celebrate your victory, give me your weapon and I will take care of this trash, sir. Your position is now too elevated to do this work." Jack held out his open palm to receive the weapon. "If you will permit me, sir?"

The prisoner, pleased to hear himself being acknowledged as a leader, shoved the weapon into Jack's hands. He turned and raced away toward the riot to claim his victory.

Jack pointed the weapon at Guard Gene and waited.

Dust billowed. Shouting could be heard in the distance. Once that prisoner was out of sight, Jack lowered his weapon.

"This is my only chance," Jack pleaded with Gene. "Please understand, Guard Gene." Jack carefully put the SP weapon down on the ground, maintaining eye contact with the guard as he stood up slowly.

"I never saw you," Guard Gene stated as he pointed toward the wall.

He pushed a button on his uniform and the solid wall opened to reveal a dark narrow corridor beyond. "Keep going straight no matter what. After a while, you'll see a door. It's an emergency escape. Good luck."

He picked up the weapon, walked right past Jack, and headed toward the sound of chaotic shouts.

Jack turned to watch Gene leave. Should Jack follow the original path he had planned to take? Should he trust this guard's offer to help him escape or was Guard Gene sending Jack into a trap?

Time was running out. The opening was beginning to close.

He had to act.

5 CHAPTER Year 2032: Morning After Earthshake (Continuous Ch 37)

The repairs the sisters worked so hard on at the Widow's Cloister had all fallen apart in last night's Earthshake. Huge cracks now tore through the walls and pathways. Plates in the kitchen had been tossed out of cupboards, and now lay shattered across the floor. Simple icons of faith hung askew on the walls. Their first order of business this morning was to attempt to bring order to the mayhem.

Elder James galloped furiously through the cloister gates straight up to the Eldress.

"These walls," Elder James shouted to the Eldress as he dismounted, "will not protect you, the widows, and the sisters, any longer."

Wringing her hands the Eldress replied, "But, what can we do?"

"I have prayed," said Elder James, "and am compelled to tell you that I sense danger is nearby. The AnCors have escaped from the Men's prison. This Cloister is the nearest building to the prison. I believe those rebels will try to take it. Please, Eldress, all of you must pack your things quickly and come with us to the Monastery."

"But, we are sisters and widows, Elder James. We cannot stay with you in your monastery."

"Please, please," Elder James interrupted, "I feel strongly that you all must come with us now. We can plan how to rebuild this place later, but you all must leave this Cloister at once! Please!"

"But, did not the Earthshake also

damage your Monetary as much as our little Cloister, Elder James?" Eldress protested.

"No, we are built on rock, Eldress, a good distance away, and we suffered very little damage to our structure."

Biting her lip, Eldress nodded with knitted brow to Elder James, who hurried outside the walls to where Earth Farmer's horses and carts were gathered, waiting. Elder James was hopeful that the Eldress, a practical woman, would lead her charges to the safety of the Monastery.

Eldress notified the women inside to halt repairs, grab what they could quickly, and leave with the Earth Farmers who were already waiting outside to assist them.

Queenie stood for a moment, gazing back at her garden. Her home. All that she knew. And, now she was forced to abandon this lush haven which she had tended so lovingly for the last two years. So many plants lay crushed under chunks of wall, which had fallen from a nearby façade, during the Earthshake.

Since Queenie could not take the produce with her, she ran into her storage area and grabbed the jars of seeds she had been collecting from previous harvests.

As Eldress hurried the ladies along, she called to the women, "Gather only the necessities for travel to the monastery..."

Then to Elder James, she beckoned, "Please help me pack these up carefully." She indicated the holy relics, "I don't want any of those sinful AnCors to take what is holy and profane it or sell it to finance their activities. We shall be ready to leave within the hour."

Elder James and the Eldress gingerly packed the sacred items as quickly as possible. Elder James signaled for the other men to help bear the weight of these fine objects and carefully load them onto the carts.

Some of the women had packed their belongings themselves, others needed the assistance of the men to help them carry bags to the horses. Finally, the cloister's residents and meager belongings were loaded and ready to depart.

Queenie was one of the last to climb into a cart. While running toward the horses, she had searched her pockets for two bullet-ridden quilting squares, now cleaned, bearing only faint blood stains. The laundered cloths were carefully folded. Seeing this quilt sample always gave her comfort for some reason. The threads binding the squares together were loose from wear.

"Hurry, Child!" Eldress shouted at Queenie who immediately increased her speed, short-cutting through her own inner courtyard garden. With sad reluctance she glanced back at all the beautifully ripe unharvested food she had to leave on the bushes and dwarf-sized trees.

What Queenie didn't notice was that as she ran, hastily trying to return the squares to her pocket, only one square of fabric made it.

The weakened loose threads binding the two squares finally unraveled, detaching them. One square fell away, fluttering down, snagging onto a low branch like a tiny flag of surrender.

Queenie scurried to the cart and hopped in.

6 CHAPTER- Year 2032: Two Days After Earthshake (Continuous Ch 38)

Fortunately, Jack Courtly, having so far eluded detection, stumbled toward the faintly lit opening that appeared from time to time at the far end of the tunnel. Feeling his way along rough earthen walls, he had serious qualms about the consequences he could expect for attempting to escape. He hoped, as he chose one dark path over another, that with each decision he was not getting himself hopelessly lost as he made his way through the claustrophobic narrow twists and turns. Pushing through overgrown shrubs and fallen debris which had, by this point, long hidden the exit from view, Jack cautiously dragged himself, at last, out into the dark, and was greeted by a clear bright moon. He slowly stood up to inhale the cold night air. Was he, in fact, now a free man?

In the distance, several miles away, he could discern the outline of a building on the dark horizon. He suspected it might be the Cloister. Exhausted from his long crawl through underground tunnels, Jack was thankful he had chosen to follow Guard Gene's escape route.

He looked around, shocked to see how far he had come from the prison and the jurisdiction of the guards. Nobody seemed to have followed him. He took a long deep breath.

After hours of walking across the desolate wilderness, Jack was thankful to see, that he had finally arrived at the gates of the Cloister.

Unmistakable.

He was exhausted.

Once teeming with the happy busy day-to-day routine of the widows and sisters, this rambling stone structure was now deserted and in shambles from the Earthshake. Just that morning, all the women had fled.

Jack walked quietly.

"Hello?" Jack called gently, but was greeted with silence.

He pulled the gates of the cloister closed behind him. Feeling dizzy from hunger, he stumbled into the inner courtyard to find the apple trees that Queenie had not finished harvesting.

Hungrily, Jack devoured the apples. He saw a well, and cranked the drum with a thick rope wrapped around it. He stopped cranking when something caught his eye.

Nearby, a Bible had been left on a bench. Opening it, he read on the inside cover "Property of Sister Jane, Widows' Cloister-Western Region." Respectfully, her replaced the Bible.

He returned to the well and continued to haul up the bucket of cool sweet water. He took a thirsty gulp. So refreshing. At least this had not been polluted from the Earthshake.

He sat down to recover on a small stone bench near the portico by the inner courtyard. Shafts of white moonlight sliced through the ornate filigree rooftops.

Jack closed his eyes, "Dear God. I know you have not heard from me in a while. I've always known what to do next, but...but...Please. Give me direction, now. Please."

He opened his eyes, feeling the chill evening breeze through his scraggy beard and torn prison clothing.

With shifting clouds in the evening sky, Jack saw one moon beam illuminating a branch in the inner courtyard. Something fluttered, catching his notice. It seemed cloth-like, waving. It didn't seem to be firmly attached to any garden plant.

Why was it there? He stepped closer to investigate.

Upon inspection, he saw a single quilt square, punctured by bullet holes and streaked with faded blood stains that hadn't quite washed out.

He recognized the pattern.

Two years earlier, Ruth Lantz, Earth Farmer, demonstrated for his child, Ace, how stitching two halves together would form the unique beginning to a quilt pattern.

The recollection of this memory physically winded him, and he sank to the ground, holding the fabric. The day he had seen this pattern, was the last time he saw his wife. It was the pattern Queenie had created especially for Ace.

2030 seemed so long ago.

Trying to control the wave of emotion which hit him hard, tears welled up as he stared at the tattered scrap. Then he shoved the cloth into his shirt.

With a surge of adrenaline, and realizing the rubble-filled building was abandoned, he carefully and quickly moved through the empty rooms, finding a cloth bag along the way. Rapidly, he stuffed the bag with what supplies he could find in the Earthshake aftermath.

He wondered where the sisters had gone. Had the woman who looked like Queenie gone with them?

Jack caught a glimpse of himself in a reflective surface. His beard was worse than unruly. No wonder that woman had been frightened.

He found a sharp knife in the kitchen, and was about to groom himself, when in the distance, he heard a noisy caravan approaching. Could it be AnCors in their loud lumbering wheeled gasoline vehicles? Were they really coming up the road toward the Cloister?

He could shave later! He threw the blade into his bag.

Checking to make sure he had the quilt square in his pocket, Jack pulled the bag up onto his shoulder, hoping he could get away under the cover of darkness before whoever it was, arrived. He knew what AnCors would do to him if they found him here.

7 CHAPTER Year 2036: Throne Room (Continuous Ch 39)

So many construction workers swarmed over the castle grounds, that there was scarcely room to move. Various groups were busy, often bumping into each other. Workers shouted over the buzz of equipment motors. Banging. Drilling. Sawing. Spilling. Falling.

Everything caused noise.

The only sound a guest might not hear was that of wildlife, since by now they had all been frightened away.

Skipper Courtly threw cost and caution to the winds as he was anxious to get that castle back to the state it was in when legend rumored powerful spirits were strongest haunting his dungeon.

In the throne room, scaffolding flanked every wall. Friezes were being mounted and frescos were being restored.

Of all the rooms in the castle, the throne room was the most lavish and nearly completed. This is where Skipper Courtly wanted to do his entertaining and intimidation.

Skipper had his priorities and his image to maintain.

In the corner of the throne room stood a simple desk. Skipper made it very clear that such ugly recycled refuse should never be near the throne once the room was ready for use. In the meantime, his son, Pip wanted it there and used it as a desk. Barely in his twenties, Pip was now taking on a more mature role by looking at the record of invoices and bills associated with this construction project. He soon realized, each expenditure chipped away at his inheritance.

Pip leaned back in his chair, his impish mischievousness was gone. He took off his glasses and cleaned them with the hem of his shirt and replaced them on his nose. Then, he reviewed the numbers one more time.

He rubbed his forehead. It seemed that his father may have been spending more than they had.

Was that possible?

Pip turned around in his chair to see his father happily inspecting the décor being installed in the throne room. Skipper was quite precise with his instructions and most particular about where a glass display case should be placed. A little to the left. No, up a bit. No, no, no. to the right, now – just two inches. That's it. No! no. no. Pip heard the monologue of orders continue as his father went on berating his workers.

Pip waited until his father clapped his hands, indicating that the display case was in the correct location and ready to be permanently mounted. Smiling, Skipper unwrapped an old violin which he planned to house in the display case, once it was anchored. Gingerly, Skipper traced the violin with one finger, as he impatiently waited to place the instrument into its new home.

Abruptly, Pip spoke up, almost frightened by the obsessive focus his father was displaying about the violin.

"Dad, you are acting ridiculous. This renovation is costing too much. Do you realize that with the money you now owe, we could have purchased a few vacation homes which would already be decorated and furnished?"

Skipper picked up the instrument and began plucking at the strings. Being unable to hear the delicate sounds with the boisterous construction in the background, Skipper brought the violin body up to his head so he could pluck the strings next his ear.

"Don't tell me what to do," Skipper snapped, annoyed. "It's not your money.

It's mine. I'm the skipper. I'm the captain of this voyage. I decide how much to spend and on what."

"Dad," Pip started with a softer tone, "You don't even know how to navigate a yacht. You hire people for that. You're really not a skipper, at all."

Still plucking the strings, Skipper's words drifted away from the point Pip was trying to make, "Isn't she beautiful? She sounds so haunting. I wonder if she could lure the castle spirit..."

"You're losing it!" Pip barked. "Would you put that thing down. There are no ghosts, here! We need to worry about finances!"

Shouting with a ripe fury, Skipper Courtly scolded, "Don't you take that tone with me, son! I can summon great powers from the universe at will! I can do what I like, Pip, when I like!"

Pip quickly grabbed a device from the desk and walked quickly to his father, shoving the display of numbers right in front of his face.

"Dad! It's a house of cards! Look at this debt. And these are estimates for more work you want done and changes you keep making to your own design. That inheritance is not money in the bank. Everything in the castle you've bought using Uncle Jack's will as collateral. But, you know you don't have the money, yet! You are spending what you hope to have. Not what you actually have."

Incensed, Skipper's face turned deep crimson. The workers around them paused, watching, anticipating the shouting match that was about to erupt. Then Skipper suddenly stopped, as if a switch had been flipped off. Gently, Skipper dismissed his son's concerns and resumed plucking the violin. "It's a technicality. When your Uncle Jack is finally declared legally dead, we'll get that money."

The workers went back to their jobs.

"Dad. There is nothing to prove here. This isn't some fraternity dare. Why not wait until you get confirmation that Uncle Jack's will is ready to pay out?"

Skipper started humming a tune to the stings he plucked on the violin. Triumphantly, he stated, "I have been patient for almost seven years. That money should have been mine all along. Your Uncle Jack was weak. He needed to move aside for a true leader. Me."

Skipper picked up a bow and started to play the instrument. His face expressed a proud experienced performer, but what came out of his violin crescendoed into a frantic Valkyrie-like storm of screeches and whines clearly revealing the hand of an untrained musician.

"A leader?" Pip shouted at Skipper to compete with the construction noises and loud violin sounds. "Maybe you can use some of your newfound supernatural powers to pay off some of these debts! At this rate, Dad, we won't be able to eat in the employee cafeteria. Do you realize that shops won't accept my good Courtly name for credit anymore? I can't buy stuff anymore! All the shops know we are spending what we don't have! What are you going to do about it, Dad?"

"I did what I had to about Uncle Jack, Pip," Skipper said as he continued to play the violin.

"Had to?" Pip repeated perplexed, cringing at the music his father played. "What does that mean?"

8 CHAPTER Year 2036: Sarah's Desk Mid-Summer (Continuous Ch 40)

Sarah meant it when she said she wanted the new student interns to actually acquire valuable skills during their apprenticeship at Courtly Corporation. The feedback she got from the students was that they all found it valuable to meet with Sarah on a regular basis and discuss work related issues. Encouraged by this informal survey, Sarah made an effort to set aside her already busy schedule to include weekly meetings with each intern.

The last appointment Sarah had at

Courtly Corp that afternoon was with Alexandra, who waited just outside Sarah's tiny glass-walled office, clutching a simple folder.

Sarah was at her desk, concluding her conversation with another student.

While Alexandra waited outside, Sarah saw the Earth Farmer boy, Joshua, approach Alexandra, speak briefly, and then leave. Sarah noted the friendly manner in which Alexandra greeted Joshua. As Sarah ended her meeting with the student at her desk, she thought it nice that an Earth Farmer boy like Joshua was making friends with the other interns.

"Alexandra, you are next. Saving the best for last," Sarah smiled.

It had been a long day and she was ready to go home, but she had made a commitment to speak with the students and she only had one more to go.

Alexandra cautiously approached and then sat down, stiffly.

Sarah smiled and waited for Alexandra to speak, which she did not.

"So, Alexandra," Sarah started after taking a deep breath, "You and I have been having these weekly status meetings, yet you never offer any comments. So, do you have any today? Or would you like to conclude our meeting?" Sarah smiled.

"Everything is fine, Miss Paradise. But, there may be one issue I could discuss." Alexandra's voice trailed off, but Sarah had heard the student's full sentence.

"That's why I'm here. To help. What work concerns do you have?" Sarah rested her chin in the palm of her hand as she reached for a writing instrument to take notes.

Alexandra didn't move, nor say a word.

Sarah put the writing implement down, folded her hands, and smiled at Alexandra, waiting.

"Um," Alexandra started, "I found this folder mixed in with some old paper files

I had to alphabetize. It looks confidential. I figured you'd know what to do with it." She pushed the folder across the desk to Sarah, then sat back in her chair, still anxious.

"Sure, it's probably mis-filed." Sarah took the folder.

Furtively looking to make sure nobody else could hear, Alexandra leaned in and quietly said, "There was an agreement between Earth Farmer elders and this corporation to store all toxics far away from Earth Farmer lands and irrigation waters. The document in that folder shows Courtly Corp is violating their own contract."

Sarah opened the file folder, "I'm really not aware of any such agreement, but if you are concerned, you could talk to one of the corporate attorneys."

Upon closer examination of the folder's contents, Sarah's eyes opened wide. Alexandra, seeing the reaction, stood up.

"Thank you, Miss Paradise, for looking into it. I need to ride a bus to the hospital, now." She headed to the exit.

"Oh? Are you not feeling well, Alexandra?"

"I am well, Miss Paradise. I volunteer at the hospital, you see. Good day." With eyes downcast and a quick curtsy, Alexandra left, allowing Sarah the time to become engrossed in the contents of this folder.

Sarah didn't notice that Pip had tip-toed in. He placed a lumpy hand-blown glass object that may have been intended to be recognizable on her desk, causing Sarah to sharply inhale in surprise.

"I just made that for you, Sarah. Surprise!" Pip smiled, "It's the end of our work day. So, it's time for a bite of dinner. C'mon. It will be my treat."

Startled, Sarah slammed shut the folder she was reading, which accidentally caused the object to roll off her desk, and break once the thin glass hit the floor.

Flustered, Sarah turned to Pip, "Oh! It broke so easily. Thank you, Mr. Courtly, uh. Pip... for the gift."

She quickly pushed her chair aside and began picking up shards glass from the floor. "But, I. Um. I still have my intern status reports to complete, so I thank you for the offer, but I really must get them done on time."

Carefully placing the bits of glass in her wastebasket she continued, "I am so disappointed it broke. It was very thoughtful of you..."

Sarah cleaned up the broken object, then started straightening her desk, trying to conceal the folder she was just reading.

"It's all right, Sarah," Pip consoled. "It didn't take long. I mean, I can whip out another one pretty fast. So, let's go."

Pip acted as if he simply didn't hear Sarah's polite refusal. He sat down on her desk, right on top of the file Alexandra had given her.

Sarah said nothing.

"Well," Pip feigned defeat, "If you gatta work, you gatta work. By the way, did you send the Tinley file to Europe? They are in a different time zone than we are."

Sarah looked confused. Pip picked up a folder marked "Tinley" from one side of Sarah's desk and handed it to her.

"I'm sorry, Mr. Courtly, uh, Pip. I was about to file those. I already redmailed them earlier today." Sarah glanced nervously at the folder Pip was sitting on.

"There was a problem, Sarah. They asked us to send it again and you know I can't figure out how that redmail thing works. C'mon, darling. Deal with it now before they worry in Europe. I'll wait here for you."

Pip shoved the Tinely papers into Sarah's hand. Reluctantly, she made her way to the door, opening it. Sarah didn't notice that Pip had picked up the file that he was sitting on and started to read it.

Before Sarah closed the door behind her, Pip stopped her with, "Uh Miss Paradise. Wait a moment."

Slowly, she turned around to face him, biting her lip, "Sir? Uh, yes? Mr. Courtly. I mean, Pip?"

He held up the file that Alexandra had given her only moments earlier and peered at Sarah over the rim of his glasses.

Softly, he asked, "Where did you get this, Miss Paradise?"

9 CHAPTER Year 2036: Hunternet Wondernet (Continuous Ch 41)

Library always served up a portion of solace to Sarah when she had to check her facts. Cautiously, she sat at a table with her chair against the wall, facing out so that nobody could surprise her from behind. In front of her lay paper reports, books, and newspapers. She turned pages wearing white cotton gloves, so the natural oils from her fingertips would not sully the paper.

Using a hand held device, she was intently focused on taking notes. Whenever she found a subject she was interested in, she turned eagerly to the page indicated only to find that the information had been heavily redacted. It was as if a wide-tipped black marking pen blotted out entire paragraphs, leaving only a few irrelevant words un-inked.

"Why didn't they just burn the book," Sarah said to herself as she flipped through the pages.

Reaching into her bag, Sarah brought out a magnifying glass. It was something she found at an antique store years earlier. She held one book up to the light, adjusting the angle of the page and was able to read a word through the black blot.

Sarah jotted down a note. This may take longer, but she was determined to get the information she needed.

Bjorn walked over to her, also carrying books. He sat down and donned a pair of white cotton gloves. What he opened up also was redacted. He shook his head as he tried to glean some information and also take notes.

Hushed, Sarah spoke softly to Bjorn, "Do you remember reading that there used to be systems that could look up information in a second?"

Whispering, Bjorn replied, "You mean hunternet?" He continued reading.

"I think it was called wondernet."

Bjorn pushed the book aside and looked at Sarah, "Hunternet. Because you had to hunt for information that wasn't censored. Then, pieces of the hunternet were sold off to different corporations. You could only search on what that corporation permitted, so the concept and technology fell apart and stopped working. Hunternet."

Sarah thought for a moment before responding, "I remember being taught that it had to be shut down because all that uncensored information coming at us so fast caused mental illness."

Casually, Bjorn tossed out, "Whatever..."And he resumed his reading.

Sarah picked up a pile of old dusty papers from the floor and placed them on the table in front of her. These records were also censored.

"Even if the wondernet was dangerous to my mental well-being, I sure could use it right now..."

Surprised at finding something in his book, Bjorn said, "Hey, look at this!"

Sara leaned over to see what Bjorn had found, "Is that even possible?" she asked.

10 CHAPTER Year 2036: Castle On The Lake The Next Morning (Continuous Ch 42)

"I can't believe I got here before the construction crews arrived," Bjorn said to himself as he walked past parked construction trucks dotted along the path leading to the castle's massive entry doors.

He heard no sounds of drilling.

Pausing for a moment to gaze at the placid lake, he noticed a small boat. It looked as if some fisherman had dragged the boat up onto the narrow beach and left it. Bjorn reasoned that it must be fun to bob around the water without any deadlines looming overhead.

Sammy, Bjorn's editor, wanted more content for the Lifestyles section of The Daily Memo, so Bjorn had to write up another article about Skipper and his remodeled castle. The deadline for that story was approaching fast just when Bjorn would rather be on a boat.

He continued to walk toward the castle entrance.

Bjorn saw Skipper Courtly hurrying toward him, obviously anxious to speak.

"Mr. Esterday! You are just in time to see the mystery of my castle dungeon!" Skipper's pudgy fingers were spread wide as if his hands exuded magic.

"Dungeon? You mean basement?" Bjorn asked.

"Dungeon. Spirits only live in dungeons, my good man. Today I select you to document how I will become the first man to harness the power of all this."

Skipper stepped around in a wide circle with arms out-stretched as if he were trying to inhale the entire world into himself, and ordered, "Follow me, Mr. Esterday."

Bjorn, reasoned that Sammy had never specified exactly what angle to take on the story so, smiling to himself, the Lifestyles reporter followed Skipper inside the castle and down to the mysterious basement.

11 CHAPTER- What will happen next?

Skipper Courtly is remodeling a castle he has just purchased for himself. Already the acknowledged leader of society, is he feeling that he still must prove that he is in fact - the king- of Courtly City? Does that mean he feels insecure about his power or position or simply that he wants to keep impressing others with his status?

Glimpsing into the Widow's cloister, we wonder if their secluded lifestyle would allow any exploration outside of the walls to see what really happened on that train back in 2030.

Being in prison when he does not deserve it may make Jack Courtly complacent and willing to accept his new surroundings, realizing that in prison his brother cannot get to him and kill him. But will Jack's personality keep him complacent knowing an injustice is being ignored? Or will Jack feel compelled to right that wrong?

As Bjorn is exposed to the throne room at Skipper Courtly's residence, will he also be blinded by all that wealth and power, or will his core sense of honor make Bjorn dig more than a little deeper into the story?

How will Sarah and Bjorn pursue their research when the society of Courtly City has locked away access to information so completely that neither Bjorn nor Sarah can even remember how the process of information retrieval was once designated. Was it Hunternet or Wondernet...or internet?

୫ To Be Continued... ଔ

12 Did You Know

How do Force Fields work?

Physicist, Ruth Bamford, at Rutherford Appleton Labs in Diodcot, England, several years ago – in 2008-, published in the journal *Plasma Physics and Controlled Fusion* .

She and her team fired a plasma beam at the speed of Mach 3 at a magnetic force field. Almost all the particles in the beam deflected off the force field.

Bamford thought that if you create a small bubble of this field, you could theoretically send astronauts to Mars safely inside that bubble.

There is a school of thought that an object, like a planet, wouldn't need the force field to surround the entire globe. Instead, scientists could create a bubble defense that would act, for example, like a bat to smack away threatening asteroids.

That means that the force field is used as a defensive repellent instead of an offensive bubble shield. But, more experimentation is ongoing.

So, would the technology of force fields become commercialized and commonplace to the point where real estate agents would use it to protect vacant homes from intrusion?

Is it possible to have a magnetic force which could withstand Mach 3 laser beams and ward off humans trying to trespass over the invisible border?

Mach 1 is the speed of sound in air. This is approximately 750 miles per hour, assuming the temperature outside is about 50F. Mach 3 is three times the speed of sound in air.

The Austrian physicist, Ernst Mach, is for whom the term "MACH" was named.

Have you ever considered why some people seem to get star-struck around a famous person? In EDGES, we see that some people treat the members of the Courtly family differently because they are essentially local celebrities.

Why does this happen?

Professor Cialdini (CHAL-DEEN-IE) at Arizona State University studied the phenomena of BIRGing and CORFing.

BIRGing (Basking in Reflected Glory)

This means that even if there is no personal history with the celebrity, an ordinary person will make an imaginary association with the celebrity. An example would be, when a sports team wins, the fans shout, "My team won."

CORFing (Cutting Off Reflected Failure)
This means the opposite. People will dis-associate and remove themselves as far as possible from somebody who has failed. If "that person over there" has experienced disaster or shame, others may avoid them because they might feel that failure would be contagious and infect them.

In other words, if a team loses, then the fans of that team will dis-associate themselves from that team. The words selected by the fan may say something akin to "They lost" rather than "We lost".

Another option for devoted fans would be to remain loyal to the losing team or celebrity, but make excuses for them and their failure by blaming something else. Blaming something outside of the control of the team which lost, such as bad weather, is another form of CORFing. This means the fans would move away from the source of failure as if it were contagious.

Some celebrities may understand this fan-behavior. They may count on BIRGing to be very strong and assume their wealth and status will allow others to forgive their bad actions.

In EDGES, Skipper Courtly is assuming BIRGing will encourage people to want to be with him no matter how he behaves because he has sufficient power and wealth. Skipper may assume that those impressed by his success want to be close to him so they will "catch the success" and so Skipper thinks he can behave poorly and still convince others to work for him gratis.

.

ABOUT Wynter Sommers

Wynter Sommers is the pseudonym for an American writing team, which harnesses multiple skills in technology, research, and education. Formally trained with a PhD in Education, Wynter Sommers blends academic classroom experience, with corporate sophistication, and a passion for developing more effective student insights.

Wynter Sommers has taught classrooms of enthusiastic children. She has a heart to inspire creativity and develop critical thinking skills, all to encourage students to make wise choices in life. She wants to impart the talent of honing one's skills in self-reliance and collaborative team work. Despite any environmental barriers outside of an individual's control, Wynter Sommers wishes to impart the message that genuine hope, love, and peace can help us overcome obstacles, and cement friendships. Wynter Sommers hopes you enjoy the other *Bjorn Esterday Was not Born Yesterday* stories in this series.